Esma Rose

By

TL KATT

A story from the Winter Thrillz Collection.

This book is a work of fiction. Any characters or events are purely figments of the author's imagination.

Esma Rose

Copyright © 2020 TL Katt
ISBN: 978-1-951017-11-8
Cover Design: TL Katt
Editor: Dawn Lewis

Published by Books by Elle, Inc.
225 College Dr. #65504
Orange Park, FL 32065
www.elleklass.weebly.com

Chapter 1

Esma stood at the crosswalk. The light on the other side flashing red. Her eyes fixed on the light until it blurred. She wrestled with her thoughts. *Was she too hard on him?* She and her boyfriend got into a fight. Esma left and

now, moments later,
stood in front of the
red hand light, staring
at it.

When they fought
it was always petty.
*Was she petty and a vain
vixen?* He called her
one and it angered
her. She was a one
man at a time gal and
it was important for a
woman to maintain
her youth and always
look presentable.

The street lights
glowed above her,
shining onto her

plaited auburn hair hanging beneath her white hat. She wore a long white leather coat matching her hat and knee-high mahogany boots. The chilly air flushed her cheeks and nose but she didn't notice the cold.

Cars beeped and honked as they zoomed past while she stood staring at the light. Snowflakes fell softly, dropping onto her and the ground.

"Are you okay?"

She zoomed out of her thoughts and glanced at the man next to her. The muscles beneath his shirt defined enough to see their outline through the loose-fitting button-up shirt he wore. His slacks, made of lightweight material, were crisp and ironed.

His face edged with a strong jawline

and his lips full, but not too full. A well-manicured mustache beneath his straight nose. Sandy brown hair streaked with gray covered his head and was neatly trimmed above his ears. But his eyes were his most striking feature. They were a piercing brown that smiled warmly at her.

"I will be," she responded.

He pressed the walk button and the

blinking red hand changed to a solid white person. They crossed the street.

"You stood in front of that light several minutes. Are you sure everything is fine?"

She adored gentlemen and thought again of her boyfriend and their silly arguments. A smile tugged at the corners of her lips. "I got into a little disagreement with a friend and now I'm overthinking it."

"You can never overthink a problem with a friend and it's never too late to make everything right again," he stated, walking in stride with her.

"This time it is," she answered with a hint of sorrow.

"How's that?"

Esma ignored his question. "This is my house. Thank you, uh… I never got your

name," she said,
brushing a white
gloved hand along his.
   "Gracen Halinger.
A beautiful lady
should never walk
home alone." He
smiled and watched as
she walked up the
stairs to her house.
   She strolled inside
and flicked on the
light, setting her keys
on the small table
beside the doorway.
She peeled off her
coat, gloves, and hat,
hanging them in the

closet, then shifted
and cautiously
stepped into the living
room. Her boyfriend
lay on the couch, his
eyes closed and chest
still. She leaned close
to him and didn't feel
his breath. "Honey."
She gently shook his
shoulder. His arm
dropped off the side
of the couch,
touching her
abdomen.

Registering he was
dead, she screamed!

Chapter 2

The gentleman didn't hesitate upon hearing her scream and ran up the steps to her home, taking them two at a time with his long stride. He burst through the door, following her screams. She was kneeling on the floor, her brown eyes huge and tears falling across her cheeks. Laid out on the couch was an olive-skinned man with dark coffee hair and a neatly trimmed matching mustache.

He rushed towards her, eying the man. "Is he--."

She cut him off with a whimper, "Yes."

"Call 911," he demanded as he grabbed a poker from

the fireplace and
stalked the house. The
living room led back
to the hallway. It was
long. Across from
him was a dining
room. A bouquet of
roses in the center of
the table set inside a
crystal vase. The
room was empty and
led into a kitchen. The
square room
contained a breakfast
nook and island, pots
and pans hung above.
All still and clear, he
went back into the

hallway, peeking into the living room. Still squatted, she was on the phone.

He sighed, assuming she was on the phone with a 911 operator. The rest of the house contained two bedrooms, a hallway bath and master bath with a large garden tub. Candles were placed around it and their scents lingered in the air even though not lit. He cleared each of the rooms and closets. Convinced no one else was in the house, he returned to her.

Sirens blaring told him she'd called and they would be in the home within minutes. "The house is clear," he said as he placed the fire poker back in its place.

"Thank you," she managed with a shaky voice.

She stood in a royal blue dress that hugged every soft

feminine curve of her body. The color brought out the red in her hair and the deep russet in her eyes. She was a beautiful woman, more so than any woman he'd laid eyes on. His urge was to take her in his arms and sweep her into his embrace. He suppressed the urge and grabbed her supple hand, caressing it in his. She gazed into his eyes.

The policeman rang the doorbell and hollered in a firm voice, "Ms. Rose."

"Come in, please," she responded, dropping his hand and entering the hallway.

The policeman introduced himself as John Neelmeger. He wasn't taller than five foot six, with a bell-shape. His small eyes set inside a face of dough and thick salt and pepper hair greased back but not enough to cover the natural wave. He took Esma and Gracen aside as his partner checked the house and the paramedics confirmed the body was DOA.

Gracen didn't leave, but answered all the questions and listened while she responded to their inquiries. It was her boyfriend lying dead on the couch. There were no signs of forced entry and no marks or blood, nothing that gave any clues to how he died. After the autopsy they'd have a better clue what killed him, but they were assuming nature took its course early for him as he wasn't more than thirty.

Only an hour earlier they'd gotten into an argument and she left on a walk. That's when Gracen found her staring at the light, snowflakes diving from the sky and puddling around her boots. His heart leaped from his chest when he spotted her.

Her oval face and red pouty lips made it impossible for him not to reach out to her. "You can't stay here. Let me take you to a hotel."

Her russet eyes shifted, meeting his. "Thank you. Let me grab my coat."

He nodded and held her coat as she slipped her arms inside the sleeves and gracefully tugged her gloves over her hands and placed her hat on at an angle that drove him wild. He didn't place her over twenty-five, while he appeared at least fifteen years her senior.

The snow now inches high and still falling would make the walk uncomfortable, so Gracen hailed a cab and the two squeezed into the back seat. She sat like a lady with her back straight against the seat and her hands folded in her lap.

"Stop at the Royale please," said Gracen to the driver. He turned and met her eyes. "Allow me to cover the cost."

"You've done so much already. I don't think I would have made it through everything without you there," she said in a demure voice.

He smiled. "It's my pleasure and I won't have it any other way. A lady such as yourself shouldn't have to face such drama alone. I will check on you in the morning." He grabbed her hand and squeezed.

"Thank you, Mr. Halinger." She squeezed his hand in

return and stepped
out of the cab.

He watched as she
entered the hotel and
called the front desk,
making sure she got
the best room and
putting her stay on his
credit card.

He lay in bed that
night unable to take
his mind off her. Her
eyes such a unique
shade of brown,
almost red mixed with
her dark auburn hair,
long legs and perfectly
proportioned body

she was a dream. His mind finally shut down enough for sleep to come but she didn't leave his thoughts.

Her soft hand took his and they walked backwards to the bed, their mouths met in a passionate kiss. Once they reached it she broke her lips away from his and unbuttoned his shirt, one by one, exposing his chest. She ran her fingers through the thin patch of wiry hair covering it, bringing her lips close she dropped kisses on it making a straight line leading to his belt.

An intense desire for her raged inside him. He'd never wanted a woman so much and felt an urgency to thrust inside her but as a gentleman he waited, brushing his hands over the back of her hair as she unbuckled

his belt and worked
the button and his
zipper, letting his
pants drop to the
floor. He tilted his
head back, his eyes
staring sightless at the
smooth cream ceiling
as she engulfed his
penis with her
moistened lips

Tenderly, he
pushed her backwards
onto the crimson satin
duvet, lifting her
cobalt gown over her
luscious legs,
displaying her nub

and revealing a neatly
trimmed patch of
sleek dark auburn
hair. He wanted
nothing more than to
please her as he
brought his mouth to
her clit and wiggled
his tongue over it,
sliding it in circles
around the lips then
driving it into her
vagina. It was syrupy
sweet like sucking on
a cherry lollipop.
Small moans of
pleasure escaped her
lips as her body jolted

with the pleasure he brought her.

"I want you," she whispered, so quietly he barely heard it.

He guided his tongue across her belly and chest as he scooted forward on the bed until his hands rested beside her shoulders and his mouth met hers. He rested the tip of his cock at her moistened entrance and brushed lightly. Her hips met his movements, driving him over the edge. He fought his craving to plunge inside her. Building the desire, he inched inside her until her tight vagina swallowed him. The walls crushing against his cock as their bodies met in waves of pleasure, whimpers and moans breaking the silence in the air.

A sudden crash awoke him. Bolting upright, his sensuous dream faded but his dick throbbing and hard as a steel blade reminded him. Juices glistened from the tip to his groin. He swiped the liquid and brought it to his nose, inhaling in her scent, causing the blood in his body to pulse and rush further into his already swelling, hardened cock. Unconcerned and clueless how her juices left his dream, he brought his finger to his mouth and sucked her syrupy juices off it. He breathed heavy and crashed back onto his pillow. Wrapping his hand around his cock, he moved it quickly up and down to relieve the pressure building in his genitals. Cum squirted from the tip as another crash blasted his ears.

Chapter 3

Officer
Neelmeger sat at his
desk cleaning up
paperwork before
going home. The last
call, and lovely Ms.
Rose, embedded in
his thoughts. There
was something about
her besides her
obvious beauty. It was
something that

attracted him so much he wanted to strip off her clothes and do her against the wall in her house at the crime scene, but it also scared him.

His cop sense told him something was askew but the evidence pointed at the man dying of natural causes. There was no forced entry, nothing was stolen from the house according to Ms. Rose, and he bore no struggle marks or blood. The young man simply died. He forced the case to the back of his mind as he wouldn't know anything until the autopsy came back.

No matter how hard he tried, her face continued to stay at the front of his mind. He settled into bed, wrapping an arm around his wife and quickly fell into sleep. A dark shadow moved over him and drifted towards his chest. Suddenly breathless, he coughed and his eyes popped open. The shadow slunk to the ground. He lifted himself out of bed and wandered to the bathroom, pouring a Dixie cup full of water.

The dark shadow moved behind him. He turned quickly and the shadow formed into the shape of a man. He watched with

wide eyes as its face
gained color and
shifted into the dead
man from his call. It
reached out a
tendrilled appendage
and wrapped it
around his arm. He
struggled against it but
the tendril became a
solid hand holding
him in a tight grip.

His gun was in the
drawer beside the bed
and he doubted it
would do much
damage against the
half-man, half-shadow

creature. His pulse quickened. The man's mouth moved but no sound came out. Its grip constricted on his arm and another tendrilled appendage grabbed his other arm and, becoming solid, squeezed him tightly. His legs free, he kicked at a shadowy leg but his foot went straight through.

"What are you?" he demanded, his pulse rushing through his body like a waterfall. He had the sudden urge to pee.

The creature's mouth moved again, but still no sound, and its brown eyes burned into his.

"Honey. John!" said the familiar voice of his wife along with the familiar shoulder shake. The one she usually reserved for the nights he snored.

He opened his eyes and blinked at her face. Short blond hair circled her round face and round blue eyes stared at him. It had only been a dream, he sighed with relief. "Was I snoring?"

"No, you were wrestling and nearly knocked me off the bed," she stated in a shaky voice.

He shrugged and raked a hand through his hair. "Long night. Let's go back to sleep."

She lay down, curling onto her side.

He rested himself against her and wrapped an arm around her but didn't go back to sleep right away. He narrowed his eyes and stared at his arm. Enough moonlight illuminated it that he distinctly saw a bruise forming in the shape of a hand.

Gracen climbed out of bed and slipped on a pair of long sleep pants. His house was a fortress and cameras angled inside and outside would tell him if anyone was inside the house. He shrugged off the thought. If any door or window was opened the alarm would be blaring as the high tech detectors were inside the house.

Taking a seat at the chair in front of the video cameras, he scanned the footage. Each one told him the same story – nothing. There was no one inside or outside -- not even a nocturnal animal. Turning from the cameras, another crash broke the silence in the air. It wasn't his imagination and sounded to be coming from the kitchen. He sucked in a deep breath and grabbed the 9mm he kept inside a drawer in the desk.

His eyes shifting as he cautiously

walked down the
stairs and toward the
kitchen. He peeked
his face around the
corner, gun out, and
scanned. A dark
shadow rested near
the stove. He flipped
the light on, gun
aimed at the shadow,
and took a deep
breath. The shadow
was a few pots that
fell out of the cabinet.
He let out his breath
and picked up the
pots. The metal hook
they hung from had

broken causing them
to fall. Chuckling, he
flipped off the switch
in the kitchen and
went back to bed.

Chapter 4

Gracen woke, his cock throbbing again from the usual morning wood. It didn't glisten in juices. He thought about the previous night and wondered if it was all a strange dream, like a dream within a dream. The only way he'd know would be to check the pans in the kitchen. Grabbing his cock, he thrust his hand over it rapidly until a flow of cum shot out of the tip. It reminded him of the previous night. He jumped off his bed, checking for any dried cum stains and, sure enough, there was a rough dried spot and he questioned again whether it was a dream or if it was real.

After changing his sheets, he moseyed to

the kitchen. The pans weren't on the floor and the cabinet was closed. He scratched his head then opened the door. The hook was firmly in place. *It was a dream, but if it was a dream how did my sheets have dried cum?* He pondered for a few seconds, then jogged back to his bedroom and to the cameras.

He ran through all the footage and saw himself jerking off,

then wandering downstairs with the 9mm but the pans were never on the floor. This gave him another idea and he checked all the time stamps but they didn't display any lapses. Without an explanation other than he must have been sleepwalking, something he'd never done, he dropped it and readied himself to check on Esma.

His mind a flurry of how he'd spoil her for the day. He felt like a giddy teenager thinking about her and his cock acted like he was sixteen as he felt it harden.

He knocked on the door of her room. She opened it, the sunlight catching the auburn highlights in her hair.

"Almost ready. I just need to slip on my shoes and coat.

Would you like to come in?"

The sensual urges rising inside him, he wasn't sure being alone in a room with her was a good idea. He wanted to ravage her body and wasn't sure he trusted himself. Her soft russet eyes smiled and he took up her offer, trying not to touch her as he assisted her with her coat.

The hotel was famous for its fine

dining and made a perfect breakfast spot. He fought a raging hard on as he watched her take delicate bites from her strawberry crepe and sip on green tea. Gracen shifted his concentration to the steak and eggs on his plate.

"The room is beautiful. I really can't thank you enough," she said in a soft voice.

"I'm happy you enjoyed the night. Did you sleep well?" he asked, cutting a slice of steak.

She wrinkled her straight nose. "Not really. It was comfortable enough, but I kept seeing his face." A tear lingered in the corner of her eye.

He wrapped a hand around hers. "I'm sorry."

Her pouty lips shifted into a smile.

"You've been so kind and you don't even know me."

He hoped to change that. "What do you say we spend the day on the ice, something to get your mind off last night?"

He eyes shifted demurely towards the table. "You've been kind enough. I couldn't accept anything more from you."

He didn't know who needed it more,

her or him. She found her boyfriend dead and it wouldn't be polite of him to hit on her after such an experience. She needed time to heal and a day ice skating and a nice dinner would do that. But the primal urges inside him needed to be near her. Their connection was like nothing he'd ever experienced.

Esma agreed to spend the day with

him. It was almost as if supernatural forces beyond the realm of the physical world wouldn't allow her to decline. Her mind drifted backwards in time to less than twenty-four hours earlier, when she'd met him. He didn't know her and owed her nothing. She was a complete stranger staring at an unchanging light. His beautiful face and kind eyes made an immediate impression on her as if something inside him was pulling her towards him.

Then there was her vivid dream of them making love. Her fingers and mouth running over his chest and his throbbing, hard cock in her hand. Normally she could control these things, but not in his case. A whistled soft melody sang through her head a moment prior to her

entering his dream.
She knew they shared
it together, although
she couldn't explain
how.

The ice on the
lake was solid as she
slid across it on her
skates. Gracen took
her hand and they
danced upon it like
two trained
professionals. He
whisked her in the air
and twirled her under
his arm. A skilled
skater he was and her
body moved in unison

with his, matching all his actions, and the rest of the world disappeared from her mind's eye.

They skated backwards, his arm wrapped around her abdomen, when the lovely melody whistled through her head. He clutched her hand and raised it above her head and spun her beneath. She spiraled out, her face just below his. Their eyes met, hers closed in anticipation of the touch of his lips against hers.

But it didn't happen and the melody halted. She opened her eyes. He cupped her chin in a hand that was far softer than any male hand she'd felt. Obviously, he didn't do manual labor and held beauty in high regard, something she shared.

His warm eyes searched hers, a

glimmer of hunger and mystery behind his irises. "You're shivering. Let me take you back to the hotel?"

Upon his words, a shiver of ice ran up her spine and she shuddered from its frigid touch. "Yes, thank you."

Chapter 5

*J*ohn
Neelmeger went back
to the previous night's
crime scene after
calling the coroner to
speed up the autopsy.
Something was amiss
and he'd figure it out.
The home was
decorated with style
and above the pay
grade of the young

man who owned it. A
simple background
check showed the
young man had never
been in trouble, not
even a speeding ticket
and his annual income
as a store manager at
Fiskins Jewelers put
him in a median
income range. No way
could he afford the
expensive furnishings
in the home.

The girlfriend,
Esma Rose, he
understood even less.
She had no income

and no record.
Nothing, literally
nothing! He couldn't
even find a social
security number on
her. He'd wait for a
deeper check to come
through before he
pointed the finger.
Name changes
weren't uncommon
but mostly in cases
where someone
wanted their identity
hidden. Such as
someone escaping a
violent situation,
witness protection, or

someone who committed a crime. He didn't toss out the last part of his thought but put it aside for the moment as he walked through the home.

He slid open the master bedroom closet to stare at men's suits, slacks, and shoes. There was nothing feminine. He rushed to the closest dresser and one by one opened each drawer, searching for something that said she lived there. All he found were men's socks, briefs and T-shirts. In the bathroom and the extra bedroom there was not one single item that said a female lived there or even visited. He'd expected to find at the least an extra toothbrush.

He jaunted outside and noted a car sat in the driveway next door. Wasting no time, he knocked on the door and was greeted by an older woman. Her brown hair, mostly gray was cut short surrounding her round face. Deep set wrinkles webbed across her cheeks and she stood with a slight hunch in her back.

Gold rimmed glasses hugged her eyes. "Can I help you?"

He introduced himself as a police officer. "How well did

you know your neighbor?"

"Oh, not well. He worked a lot and kept to himself."

"Did you ever see a woman come and go from his house; very pretty, dark auburn hair, nicely dressed?"

"No, but I'm an old woman and go to bed long before the young leave their houses for the evening…" her words hung in the air.

Vaguely, he remembered her face peering out the window as he entered the home the previous night. Maybe the commotion woke her up. He pushed his mind, trained to be observant. No, she'd been awake as light from the TV flashed behind the curtains. "If you remember anything—"

She cut him off and narrowed her eyes beneath the lenses of

her glasses making them drop to the middle of her nose, "There was something odd. Maybe not for someone so young in this generation, but recently I'd hear noises."

"What type of noises?"

"Not the kind an old lady like me wants to talk about, but grunting and moaning like the… the sexual kind." She cleared her throat.

So he was having sex. That wasn't a crime. "But you've never seen a woman go into his home?"

"That's what makes it really odd," she stated with a sigh.

Why would a young beautiful woman hide a relationship? There was only one reason he could think of, *she's married.* Double bingo: that explained why he couldn't find her name in the database. She used a phony.

He thanked the elderly lady and walked back to the young dead man's house. There he checked under all the furniture, rifled through the cabinets and beneath each cushion. Defeated, he let out a long, deliberate breath. The house contained nothing to lead him to her and he wasn't a detective, simply a beat cop. This was something he was doing on his own time because his intuition was gnawing away at his guts. The revelation he'd never find her sunk in and he turned to leave.

He clutched the doorknob that suddenly heated like a scalding pot. Yanking his hand away quickly, the dead man stood between him and the door, buzzing in and out like bad TV reception. He mouthed something

Neelmeger couldn't quite figure out until his words abruptly gained volume like someone pressed the unmute button. "Men are her prey, save him from her!"

The lights in Gracen's home dimmed automatically as he passed through the halls. He'd reset the timers after the previous night, convinced as silly as it was that maybe something, definitely not someone, had been in his home. After brushing his teeth he turned over the comforter and top sheet on his bed and slipped beneath fully nude.

He closed his eyes and waited for her to come into his dreams again. It was the only way. Her delicate face, refined features, and femininity danced across his mind as he fell into a deep sleep.

Esma rested in the large oval tub, the jets on full massaging her legs and back with their flow of heated bubbles. The only light in the room came from the candle the hotel supplied as it danced over the walls. She closed her eyes and thought of Gracen. He was more than anyone she'd ever met, but nothing like any simple man.

In her mind she drifted into his bedroom. The décor screamed masculine bachelor with functional modern furnishings and a simple green comforter resting over his sleeping body. His side and back rose and fell with each breath. She sat on the edge of the bed beside him, lifting an arm above his head and softly touching his thick salt and pepper hair.

She kissed his head and moved her lips behind his ears brushing against his skin. Her fingers maneuvering beneath the bed's coverings searching for his pleasure stick. The object that would bring her the orgasm her loins sought. A surge of wetness coated her vagina as she thought of the massive orgasm she

nearly reached. It was
her purpose, her one
desire that had been
denied her, but he was
the man who'd make
it happen.

Her juices dripped
down her legs. She
needed him. This
wasn't normal for her;
something about him
drove her wild. She
felt like a deprived
animal let loose from
its cage. Her breath
came in heavy waves
as she grasped her
chest against his flesh,

his joystick in her hand. It pulsated, growing hard and hot, pre-cum dripping from its tip. She'd never taken it this far before, always joining their dreams not bringing a man into hers. It was chancy but she pushed the risk aside and sucked the pre-cum off his tip, engulfing his large cock inside her mouth. Her hands rubbing against his soft flesh.

In his dream he moaned and she guided his fingers to her entrance and he hurriedly, as if desperate for her, found his way over her clit, gently rubbing and bringing her to ecstasy. Her breathing heavier with each touch, with each sensual moment, until she couldn't handle it any longer and neither could he.

His hands guided her onto his thick,

throbbing cock. As
she gently moved on
top of it, a series of
small orgasms jolted
her body and in the
moment she wanted
him so bad and tasted
the large orgasm. The
one that would jolt
her into a level of
frenzy she could only
imagine. She pushed
onto him but his firm
grasp around her
waist prevented her
from pressing down
and fulfilling her need.

He held her vagina at his helmet. His hands moving with her body. He shouldn't have so much control in his sleep and stop her from performing her deepest desires. Her fluids leaked over him, spilling onto the sheets as her pussy gripped tighter and tighter in waves of orgasms. She was a sensual creature and needed him now. She fought his grip. The walls of her vagina grasping him as she edged further onto his penis.

The melodious whistling, a sensual sound in itself, came back, filling her ears and his grasp tightened around her waist as their dream worlds combined in a jolt that dizzied her. The room around them changed from the bathtub she was soaking in to his bedroom. The

candlelight dancing
across the walls then
the darkness of his
unlit room.

She opened her
eyes wide, confused
about what happened.
She took a risk
because she wanted
him so badly. Her
vagina aching with
insatiable need, she
quickly thrust two
fingers into it and
caressed her breasts as
her body quaked with
orgasm and unfulfilled
desire. Her back

arching, lifting her belly out of the tub and her face beneath the water. Liquid groans of pleasure echoed inside the bathroom.

Chapter 6

racen bolted awake, her juices all over his penis and running down his hips onto the blanket around him. He hungered for her as it pulsed, pre-cum dripping from the tip and mingling with her juices. He grabbed his cock in one hand and rubbed, with the other hand he wiped her juices and licked it off until he had every drop of her liquid candy.

His hand moved with speed over his cock until cum surged from the tip. But it wasn't what he needed. His penis still erect, he continued jacking off. Guttural screams escaped and erupted from his mouth. His appetite for her unfilled. After four ejaculations, his cock finally relented. His breath heavy, he tried and almost pulled her out of the dream and into his bedroom where he wanted her.

He lifted from his bed, pulling off the sheets and tossing them into his hamper. At this rate he'd have to go shopping for sheets and a pill that worked the opposite of Viagra. His cock twitched with the thought as he turned on the cold water in the shower and stood beneath it, staring into the drain as the water cleaned away any remnants of their juices.

"Stay away from her," crippled his ears as if shouted straight into them. He stumbled and fell backwards, knocking his head against the large shower tiles. The last thing he saw as his world went black

was her dead
boyfriend, who he
doubted anymore was
actually her boyfriend.

John Neelmeger
swirled his bagel in
the egg yolk before
lifting it to his mouth.
He didn't know what
to think of the image
he'd seen and he
didn't believe in
ghosts, but energy
surges maybe. *Is it
possible for a human body
to have a surge of energy*

after death? What are you thinking? Of course not.

"Darling, you're quiet this morning," his wife stated as he chewed on a bagel.

Swallowing and washing his final bite down with a gulp of orange juice he willfully ignored her question giving her a kiss on the cheek. "I'll see you tonight," he said and walked out the door.

It wasn't anything against his wife. After

fifteen years of
marriage he'd learned
to keep work to
himself and, more
importantly, didn't
know how to explain
what he'd seen and
heard to anybody. He
wasn't even sure he
believed it himself,
but wasn't leaving
anything to chance.
The man with her that
night, a complete
stranger, had walked
her home and upon
hearing her scream
entered the house to

see her slumped on the floor next to the dead boyfriend. He'd also left a card. *Gracen Halinger, Antique Dealer.*

He dialed the number, praying it wasn't a phony. After several rings, when he was about to hang up, a voice answered.

"Gracen here."

"Mr. Halinger. This is Officer Neelmeger. Uh… from the other night. Do you have time today to meet with me?"

"I have a full schedule today with an auction…" his voice drifted off.

"Shall I meet you there?" he asked.

"No. How about I call you this evening?" Neelmeger nodded in response as expected. The man wouldn't be calling him back. In his patrol car he ran his name. 1523 Knotting Rd. West. A ritzy, high-class area. No one with an income less than nine figures a year could afford to live there. *So why was he wandering around the city the night of the murder?*

The mystery grew stranger all the time and it wasn't a case… or was it? He had enough time to check in with Judy at the coroner's office before he started his shift. They were in the same building, but he worked off the third floor and the coroner was in the basement.

The elevator doors opened and the smell of death, formaldehyde, and bleach stung his nostrils. He'd always hated coming downstairs and on most occasions never needed to unless he was doing a favor for someone else.

"Well, a visitor that dares my domain. How are you, John?"

said Judy, strapping latex gloves on her hands.

"Checking on the young man from the other night. Did you find anything?"

"He's not a priority, but I have to ask how such a young man dies so early, so I worked him in and he died of a heart attack. There are no signs he suffered heart problems and his organs are beautiful, unfortunately he's not a donor. I wish more people would check that box. Their organs aren't doing them any more good once they're dead." She sighed, her chest heaved outward.

All the talk of organs creeped him out and he understood why people didn't check that box. He planned on dying and being buried with all his organs intact. "There was nothing odd?"

Her eyes widened. "Weren't you listening? The whole thing is weird, but no sign he didn't die of natural causes. I even pulled his medical records and nothing. He was a healthy man with a strong ticker, last physical a year ago."

Her words didn't encourage him but they confirmed the sinking feeling in his gut. He was murdered and the woman had

something to do with
it.

Upstairs at his
desk, he searched for
similar deaths.
Without the clearance
and communication
of other areas he
couldn't look beyond
the city he was
employed in. While
waiting, he grabbed a
cup of coffee and sat
back at his desk. He
scrolled through the
list with his eyes. It
was much shorter
than he thought and

included two deaths
within the past four
years. In both cases
the men were in their
late twenties and
handsome according
to their driver's
licenses. Neither were
married, but *was she
married?*

Gracen Halinger
was the best bet he
had for finding her.
He grabbed his coffee
and headed
downstairs to meet his
partner who was
waiting impatiently

for him. As he was
the senior partner,
she'd have to wait.

Gracen thought
about the cop. *Wasn't
the man's death natural
causes?* He had his
suspicions due to the
past two nights, but
didn't think the cop
had the same intuition
or experience. Either
way, he didn't have
time today to deal
with him. He had
work to do.

There were real bad guys out there, ones who killed innocent people in gruesome ways. He reached out with his mind to the neighboring homes, none with less than an acre lot with forest in between. During the summer, the leaf cover would make it easy for him to hide, but with all the naked trees his car would be easier to spot unless he parked it at a vacant neighbor's house.

Luckily, the house next door was empty. Not a single brain wave, not even a small animal, showed up on his psychic radar. He pulled in and walked up the steps as if he was knocking on the door; for all purposes, it needed to look real. When no one answered, he went around the house and snuck around the back. There was no fence and plenty of trees so he dropped himself and slunk through the forest, making himself as low to the ground as possible.

He didn't need to go inside, but wanted to be close if needed to rescue the young girl locked in the basement. Finding the man's brain pattern, he attached his mind and forced his way through the gruesome memories containing chains and gore. His face cringed as he moved past them without looking harder than he needed. Entering the man's conscious thought he sent a mesmerizing brain-to-brain whistle.

At first the man fought it, his brain trying to push him out but his human mind was no match. In minutes, he had him blowing out his own brains with a gun.

Once his brain waves ceased, Gracen reached out his mind again, hoping someone heard the gunshot. He didn't appreciate entering sicko's homes and hated to make the call himself. It was much simpler and less dirty when people did that for him. In this case, someone was home behind him and already made the call.

He waited for a few minutes until the

distinct sound of
sirens filled his ears,
then got back into his
car and started the
engine. Slowly he
pulled out and eased
down the road. A
police car wailed past
him. He locked eyes
with the driver –
Officer Neelmeger.
Just his luck, but not a
problem. Erasing
minds was far simpler
than controlling them.

His brain whistled
the message, *You never
saw me here today and*

you won't pry anymore
into the young man's
death the other night. He
died from a heart attack.
He put the latter part
in for extra measure.

Chapter 7

Esma spent the day at the spa getting a facial, a full body massage, and finished with a fresh pedicure and manicure. Primping herself always erased her sexual frustration, but today it only lessened it as Gracen continued popping into her head.

After a late room-service dinner, she lay down. It was nearly eleven o'clock. Like a giddy school girl with her first crush, she closed her eyes and sought him out. She didn't bring him into her dream again, that was too chancy, instead she entered his dream conjuring a lacy negligee that barely covered her

private area and
nipples.

She landed in a
hot tub with him
suckling her breasts
above the lace on the
negligee. His fingers
pushed the lace
downward,
uncovering one of her
breasts. He rolled his
tongue around it as
unexpected moans
left her lips. Oh, she
wanted him and she
couldn't take any
more of the teasing.

She'd have him tonight.

In her hand she clutched his thickening cock and rubbed it against her leg as he nibbled away at her nipple then gently pulled down the other side and nibbled away at that one. Desire filled her up as she leaned, his instrument in her hand, and kissed his shoulders. His lips met hers and they kissed. Currents of yearning coursed through her and she moved upward, her hands resting against his shoulders.

His lips crashed against her and the tip of his cock rested at the mouth of her entrance, moving gently against it, driving her insane.

He yanked her negligee off, tossing it out of the hot tub. Bubbles beat against his back as he fought

the urge to take her
now. He wanted her
badly, had to have her
tonight. Tiny orgasms
rolled through her and
she shuddered in
ecstasy. Her defenses
were weakening, but
so were his as his lips
brushed against her
soft flesh and his
finger against her
throbbing clit. Yes,
she was nearly there.

He brought his
finger to his mouth
and licked off her
juice. More pre-cum

erupted from his swollen penis. She placed his finger back on her clit then raised it to her mouth as she sucked slowly and deliberately. It drove him over the edge. "I want you, Esma, now!"

Her pussy grabbed hold of his cock. Its walls squeezing and throbbing against it and she moaned, breathless. "I want you too, Gracen." As his penis disappeared inside her. He'd never felt any pleasure like it, causing him to ejaculate immediately.

"Oh, Gracen. Ohhhh…" she screamed, her body quivering and jerking from the intense pleasure. He almost didn't notice from the extreme pleasure he felt. His own body convulsing in waves of ecstasy. Once the initial wave ended, he continued, her walls squeezing him tight as she continued to move her hips and groan.

♥♥♥♥

The whistling melody sang through her mind as he fully entered her. His cock thickened more, causing her entire body to erupt in the most intense pleasure. His warm cum mingled with her juices and indescribable pleasure shot through her body and continued as he moved inside her. She felt her vagina pulsing around him.

"Yes, yes, oh… oh… yes, Gracen," she shouted as the most intense flood of desire released with an orgasm that rocked her body. She fell limp against his chest.

"Esma, Esma," he hollered, panicking. "Esma, I love you!" He was afraid he'd be too much for her.

Tears fell across his cheeks. He'd never loved a woman and certainly never confessed it to another, but she was something extraordinary and he meant it.

Through his tears, he realized they were no longer in his dream hot tub. They were on the floor of her hotel room. He hadn't noticed when it happened or how, but he was truly holding her in his arms.

"Esma." He kissed her lips.

A few moments later her back twitched. He laid her on the bed and smoothed the hair from her face. Her eyes rolled beneath their lids. "Gracen," she said in a whisper.

"I'm here, Esma." He kissed her forehead.

"How? What happened?" she

asked, her eyes open a slit.

"My most precious Succubus, I pulled you out of my dream."

She reached a hand towards his face and smoothed his chin with the back of it. "How? I don't understand."

"I'm not sure. I think it was our getting carried away." He kissed her soft cheeks.

"No, no, how do you know what I am?" her face cringed.

"I've been around for a very long time and seen just about everything, but you are the first succubus, that's why I didn't figure it out right away."

"What are you?" she asked, her voice intense.

"In the beginning they called us Sirens, but over time the male population moved elsewhere. The females seduce and bring harm to others, giving the name *Siren* a bad taste in people's mouths. We disassociated and prefer to help those in harmful situations. So I call myself a Whistler," he said, resting his head on an elbow.

Her head still on the bed, her dark auburn hair circling it, she rubbed her hand over his mouth. "I

love you, Gracen. You
are the man I've
waited for."

Chapter 8

Officer
Neelmeger's eyelids
drooped. It had been
a long day after
finding the young girl
chained in the
basement. Her captor
sprawled facedown, or
what was left of his
face, on the floor
dead, the gun he killed
himself with still

clutched in his hand
and brain matter and
blood splatter coating
the walls.

Knowing they'd
saved the twelve-year-
old missing girl and
returned her to her
family made him feel
warm and fuzzy
inside. It was the
image of the dead
man and the wonder
of how many other
young girls he'd
stolen, killed, and
raped that kept his

mind too fluid and active for sleep.

Yawning, he stretched then clicked off the remote and stood. A chill worked its way up his legs. He looked down and squinted his eyes in disbelief as a black mist moved upward then swirled away from him, taking the shape of a young man. The one who died of a heart attack.

"She killed me, John," he said, his

face so close it
appeared as fuzz to
Neelmeger.

His heartbeat and
breathing quickened
at the sight. He
thought to go for his
gun that rested on the
lamp table behind
him, then thought
again as he doubted it
would do much good
with a ghost. "What
are you, and what do
you want?"

"I have to tell you
so I can move on.
Esma. She came to

me in my dreams for several months. She's strong and succulent with a sexual appetite like nothing I've ever seen. From one dream to the next she worked me harder. Her hunger getting stronger and that night her lust-driven urges worked me so hard my heart gave out." His form blinked in and out then became steady.

Neelmeger scratched his head in

confusion and doubt. He must be so tired he was seeing things. "You want me to arrest someone for wild consensual sex?"

"Bars won't hold her, she's a succubus and I knew. That's why she killed me," he said, his voice so filled with static Neelmeger didn't catch the entire statement.

A blinding light filled the room, enveloping the young man. His body stretching as he fought the light long enough to say, "She's dangerous!" then he slipped away into the light and it disappeared.

Neelmeger blinked his eyes and glanced around the room. He stood beside the couch as images of Esma Rose and Gracen filled his mind and he remembered everything. The only lead he had was

Gracen's address. Throwing his coat over his sweat pants and strapping on his gun, he grabbed the car keys and headed out the door.

Gracen's house stood silent and dark. His mind was a flurry of thoughts. The succu-thing he called her couldn't be. Supernatural creatures didn't exist and neither did ghosts. What he saw was his mind playing tricks on

him. Random
thoughts that surfaced
in his tired mind
hinting that Gracen
Halinger was guilty
too. He didn't doubt
they set it up.

It was too clean.
Gracen just happens
to meet her while
taking a walk and
walks her home.
Courteously, he waits
outside her door to
make sure she made it
safely inside, then
hears her scream. The
little story gave her an

alibi and it made him appear as a stranger — someone who had nothing vested.

The problem was, why would Halinger take an evening stroll miles away from his house? And there was not one sign she occupied the house with the young man. *They screwed up,* he thought as he searched for a way inside the metal fence with pointed tips.

Walking around the house, he spotted an old tree with a branch hanging over into the other side. It looked sturdy enough to hold him even though he was much heavier than in his tree-climbing youth. The trunk was short and formed a V where other shoots branched off.

He placed his hands inside the V and hefted his weight, his chest falling

against the V as he
struggled to grasp
onto a branch and
finish lifting himself
upward. After several
minutes of struggling,
he stood with his feet
solid on the branches
of the V and climbed
onto another branch
then another until his
body hovered above a
pointed stake on the
fence. If he slipped at
all it would mean his
death. He scooted
along it on his belly,
his arms wrapped

around the thick
branch.

Once he passed
over the fence, he let
his legs dangle
downward and
dropped onto the
dead winter grass.
Pulling out his gun, he
ran-walked towards
the house. His eyes
shifting about as he
observed his
surroundings.
Reaching the back of
the house, he peeked
through the dark
windows. With no

signs of life he tried
the windows and
doors. All were locked
up tight, so he
overturned every
planter and rug
searching for a key.
Not finding one, he
cringed as he picked
up a large decorative
rock to throw it.

Something fell out
of it onto his foot and
pinged to the ground.
He picked it up and
smiled, something was
on his side. He found
the key and it worked

as he listened to the
lock click. Pushing
open the door, he
sauntered into the
house. A whining
noise caught his
sensitive hearing as he
worked his way to the
back of the house.

The noise led him
to the master
bedroom closet.
Taking a deep breath,
he thrust the door
open, gun pointing
into the closet. A wall
of TVs sprawled
above a laptop sitting

on a desk, and a chair. It didn't surprise him the man had a security system and, if anyone checked, he was in the area and heard a scream. As an officer sworn to uphold the law and protect the public, he was simply doing his job.

It was always better not to take the chance, so he unplugged the TVs and grabbed the laptop then left. He climbed back into the

tree, dropping once
he made it safely over
the fence. A siren
blared as he ran away
from the house,
computer in hand. He
caught his breath once
he made it to his car,
then drove away with
his lights off.

Once he was a
safe distance from the
house he pulled over
and flipped open the
computer, clicking
and opening his
pictures and videos.
The computer was

empty – wiped clean. Frustrated, and his lack of sleep catching up to him, he turned the lights on and pulled onto the road.

The sound of bending metal filled his ears as his car spun from the impact of the other car -- a light colored Chevy, he noted as his car spun past it into a tree, killing him instantly. A low whistle and *I told you to forget us.*

Chapter 9

Gracen held Esma's hand as they shopped at the outdoor vendors. She loved Mexico and was so grateful to find the man who could meet her sexual appetite. No more hiding in men's dreams. Until Gracen, she'd never been with a man outside the dream world, but brought unthinkable pleasure to them where she seduced them only to be unfulfilled. Over time she grew less patient with them as her sexual hunger and lack of fulfillment by mere humans left her frustrated, always having to pleasure herself after finishing with them.

She tilted her head and glanced at Gracen. The warm,

humid air surrounding them and bright sun twinkling in his eye. "I can stay here for a while."

"You can," he chuckled, happy to have the most delightful creature at his side. After over 5,000 years in existence, he'd amassed a great deal of wealth and a home on every continent. When one home became uncomfortable, he

moved onto another.
It was difficult being
immortal, constantly
moving and changing
his identity every
thirty years or so and
never making any ties.
Immortality wasn't all
humans made it out
to be. In fact, he
always considered it a
curse. Now, with
Esma by his side,
everything had
changed.

His cock twitched
as he thought of her.
Squeezing her hand in

his, he asked, "Are you ready to go back to the house?"

She knew what that meant and the thought alone made her feminine juices trickle over her thong and wet her upper thigh. She stopped walking and placed her arm around him. Standing on tiptoe, she whispered in his ear, "I can't wait that long."

She let go of his hand and slid it

between them as she felt his hardened love tool and whispered, "It doesn't feel like you can either."

He groaned as he pressed his lips against hers. "I can't. I need you now."

They ran back to the beach and finding a hidden cove, dodged inside it. She hurriedly unzipped his pants. Foreplay would come later, for now they needed each other. The tide moved in

and out over the sand,
humming a tune in
their ears. He ripped
her thong off.
Wasting no time, he
thrust his throbbing
cock inside her and
she squealed as the
first wave of orgasms
rocked her body.

Esma Rose is one story from Winter Thrillz 2, only available in ebook. Keep reading for the first two chapters of Jazzy.

Esma Rose

Jazzy

Chapter 1

I wrinkled my nose as a burst of exhaust fumes eased into it. The two cars beside me were closing distance so I quickly made my move and veered my car into the lane, squeezing between them. I always missed the turn, even after

following the same
route for the third
time this month alone.
The driver behind me
grumbled as he
flipped me off and
honked on his horn,
but I made it into the
tight space and made
the left turn onto the
familiar road. The
trees rushed past as
the mass of flowing
traffic surged forward
at speeds exceeding
fifty.

A few miles
down, I pulled into

the right-hand lane
and followed it
around to garage
parking. This part of
the trip I never
messed up. On
instinct, I ducked my
head as I entered the
parking garage,
reminding myself the
roof in my car didn't
shrink and I should sit
up. Straightening my
back, I fought the
urge to keep ducking
as my car climbed the
winding path until I
spotted a free parking

space. As a bonus it was close to the elevator that would take me on the catwalk to the airport.

The muggy Florida air hung like suspended water droplets, coating my already sweaty skin even though it was December. The air conditioner in my car quit working last week; due to limited funds and time I hadn't gotten it fixed. In Florida, when people buy cars, the one thing they're concerned about is the air. Forget new tires, brakes and leaky hoses; air conditioning was a must.

Cool air covered my sweaty skin, causing me to shiver as I stood in the line to check in. As I reached the counter I handed the lady my license and said, "To Atlanta Georgia on the 5:35 flight."

She glanced at it from under her glasses. "Jazzilynn Spencer?" she said in a question.

Jazzilynn was my legal name that I always used on airline tickets or anything legal but nobody, including my teachers throughout school, ever called me by it. I was always Jazzy. I nodded a yes.

She placed her hand on the keyboard and scrolled, making

sure to touch with the tips of her fingers and not her dangerously long finger nails, sharpened to points like tiny little daggers. Her brows arched and forehead wrinkled as she mumbled to herself.

"You said Atlanta?"

"Yes, is there a problem?" I didn't have time for this crap. Atlanta was an almost six hour drive and I needed to be there within three.

"I don't see your name. Have you ever been married, maybe booked it under a different name?"

"No."

"Let me try something else." She clicked more buttons as I waited.

A few minutes later, someone else showed up and they ogled the screen then peered at me. "I'm sorry, but you're not on this flight and it's full."

My mouth dropped. There was no way. "I booked it last night and it was half full. There's no way!"

She swiped her long auburn bangs from her eyes, displaying enormous amounts of boxy blue and lavender shadow. "I'm sorry, there's nothing I can do."

Then I remembered the

confirmation emailed after booking. I pulled my phone from my purse and opened my email, hoping my 4G wouldn't bug out on me. Luckily it didn't and I found the email, stuffing it in front of her face.

I watched her eyes with their outdated makeup move from me to the phone. She cleared her throat. "I can book you on the next flight and put you on standby for this one. If anyone misses their flight then you get the spot. It's the best I can do."

The best? I bought a ticket and am being denied its use? "I have a funeral to get to!" I stressed. Rage and anxiety swirled together as they rushed up my spine. Water glassed my eyes and soon large crocodile tears burst forth and dropped onto my cheeks. Jacob's face splintered in my mind. He'd always had my back. It was my turn to have his.

I reached over the counter, oblivious to what anyone around me was thinking or saying, and grabbed for my driver's license. Bad Makeup Job swatted at my hands as if I couldn't retrieve my own property. I swatted back as I snatched it then stuffed it into my purse and backed away, one slow step at a time.

I had a decision to make, either get in my car and make the near six hour drive to Atlanta, sweating like a sweet tea on a summer day, or wait. Neither was going to save Jacob. I shuddered as another wave of emotions washed over me. I'd drive. It was my best chance to get there.

A deep voice from behind me said,

"Miss Spencer, I need you to come with us."

I turned to see a tall man with a build as thin as the blond hair on his head. He looked like he'd fall over if I pushed him. A firm hand grasped my arm before I had a chance to respond.

I turned my head. The firm grasp belonged to a large man. His polo shirt did little to hide that his chest was bigger than mine, only all muscles. "What?" I asked through my tears.

The thin one restated his request as the strong one pulled me along. It wasn't that I was given a choice. White paint covered the walls and plastic chairs, resembling the kind seen in all public schools across the country, were in the middle of the tiny room. The strong one released his grip as the other closed the door and twisted the lock.

My tears dried up as rage alone filled every pore in my body. "First I'm kept from my flight and denied being at my friend's funeral. Now I'm locked up with stick fry and block," I spat.

"I understand you must be very upset and confused, but we need you to answer a few questions. Do you have a sister or a female cousin that you resemble?" said the thin one.

The strange question took me aback. "Why?"

"I ask the questions, not you."

"I don't know what's going on." I dumped my purse on the floor. "There's no weapons. You have no grounds to pull me back here. I want to leave now!"

The thin one sighed. "You fit the

description of someone we were warned not to let on the flight."

I narrowed my eyes. "I was denied using a ticket I paid for because I look like some felon or terrorist running around?"

The muscular one stood silent, his arms crossed over his large chest and his firm jaw clamped closed. I wondered if he had a voice. If I didn't hate him I'd admit he was attractive with his thick dark curls and silky brown eyes.

The thin one spoke again, "There is an alert for this person and if you know something you need to tell us."

"I don't know anything and I'm not dangerous. I am leaving," I stated, picking up my wallet, keys, and lipstick. *My luggage?* I thought back. I'd had it at the

counter and even
lifted it onto the scale.
"I guess you already
rummaged through
my luggage and found
it is only filled with
clothes."

The thin one
nodded. "It's been
cleared and is waiting
outside the door."

"Did you have
fun going through my
underwear?" I huffed
as I twisted the knob,
breaking the lock, and
strode down the eerie
white corridor,

wheeling my luggage behind me. I didn't turn and look but imagined the looks on their faces when they realized their little lock couldn't keep me inside.

Chapter 2

I followed
the corridor the way
they brought me.
When I came to the
door I pushed it open,
knocking it off its
hinges. The beast
inside me was loosed.
People talked and
bustled about unaware

of anything but
making their flights.

As I stepped back
into the muggy air, I
took a deep breath
and continued my
pace until reaching my
car. They'd follow me
and were probably
watching me on
security cameras. I
didn't care; let them
follow me. They'd
messed with the
wrong girl in ways
they would
understand before the
night was over.

The trees, grass, and buildings whizzed past me as I drove further away from town, hauling my ass at speeds exceeding my car's limit. It didn't appreciate that. *I'm coming Jacob, hold on,* I thought, hoping he heard me. I felt nothing in response, a void.

I am a majestic or, in layman's words, an alpha female. A panther who will one day lead the few

panthers left in
Florida. We live under
cover in our human
forms, hunting at
night in the vast
wilderness and
wetland areas that
remain. Our enemy
isn't the humans.
They are simply in the
way, annoying and
completely oblivious
to the battle that's
been waging for
centuries now.

I wasn't on the
road an hour when I
noted head lights

behind me. Through my superior vision I kept one eye peeled to the car as I hit I-16 W. Pushing my car to its limit, it flew over the pavement on the near-deserted road. The car continued to follow, so I slowed and veered off onto a back road and then another even less-traveled one, until I was deep in the woods somewhere between I-16 W and Atlanta.

I didn't doubt all of this was due to our mortal enemies: the jaguars. The battle was over territory. As our inferiors, they weren't as strong physically and couldn't change when they pleased as we could, but they did adapt better into society and into high-reaching places of authority.

I flipped the lights on as the last of the sun's light dropped

below the horizon,
following the roads
deeper and deeper
into the woods. The
headlights behind
stared like two eyes in
the night, hunting me.
Steering my car onto a
grassy area, I left the
lights on and crept
towards the trees, my
movements as
seamless as the gentle
breeze. Crouching
behind the trees, I
waited.

All this was taking
precious time, but

Jacob would understand. A black SUV passed. About a mile down, its headlights went out. Being nocturnal, I didn't need light to see three large men step out of the vehicle armed with semi-automatics.

Blowing out a disgruntled breath, I waited in my spot, blending with the trees surrounding me. They weren't jaguars because they didn't

carry guns, always
ready to take us on in
hand to hand combat.
Their clumsy footfalls
told me they were
human.

Guns poised, they
circled my vehicle.
One of the bulky
men, his wavy brown
hair and silky eyes
giving away he was
the attractive block
man from the airport.
A second one with a
smooth, bald head
and muscles
exploding from

beneath his shirt
glanced toward the
other men who
confirmed a yes nod.
Another one with
tattooed sleeves
strode behind him
and perched with his
gun at the ready. Even
a semi-automatic only
served to slow us
down. Normal bullets
would eventually fall
out, rejected by our
bodies.

I grabbed a small
branch resting by my
foot and hefted it

towards my car. It hit
the roof and dropped.
Darn, another dent.
They tilted their guns,
poised to shoot when
the bald one said, "It's
just a branch."

Tattoo squared
his shoulders and
dropped the gun to
his side. "Think she's
gone? Car trouble,
maybe?"

The bulky man
from the airport
punched his brows
and followed the tree
line with his weapon.

"No, she's hiding, out there." *He speaks! Just when I thought he was mute and damn he's clever!* I thought sarcastically. He cocked his gun to point into the woods.

The three men split up and stalked towards the treeline. I could take them out pretty easily but I'd never know what was going on. Why they were following me and why I was denied my flight? That still angered me, not only because it was Jacob's funeral, but I'd spent a fortune on a last minute ticket. Heat rose through my veins, pumping, my cat attempting to force its way out. *Deep breath, calm down.*

My ears soaked in their movements. Tattoo had harder footsteps and Baldy's were more labored, as if he'd suffered some type of knee injury. The bulky man from the airport had the most graceful steps. He was also the smallest of the buff gang.

Tattoo stalked towards me. His semi-automatic only a few feet from my face as he dropped his shoulders to avoid hitting a large, twisted branch. His eyes shifting side to side as he searched for me.

Forgive me Jacob. I picked up my feet and sprinted through the trees, my footfalls crashing against ground litter as I purposely stepped on every pile to grab his attention. I'd let them catch me. I wanted, no needed, to know for myself and my fellow panthers why they were after me.

Shifting his gun towards my direction he shouted to his buddies, "Over here guys!"

They weren't supernatural by any

means with all the noise they made and shouting like that was plain stupid. Woods housed cougars and, on occasion, a passing wolf pack. The panthers and cougars coexisted as allies, as the jaguars were greedy bastards and were attempting to move into Georgia territory as well.

This wasn't a battle between shifters, but something else. Soon

three sets of feet
pounded the ground,
wet leaves squishing
beneath their shoes as
I swerved between
trees. I couldn't let
this whole chase
appear easy, so I
dropped, tripping
over a tree root when
I heard Baldy only
feet behind me.

Scraping to stand,
I clutched the dirt and
litter then turned my
head. His gun was
pointed towards me
when Baldy's voice

boomed through my
ears. "Got her guys!"
I scooted backwards,
my eyes wide in fear,
and scrambled to my
feet, tossing the dirt in
my hands towards
him and took off
again as if in fright.
"Damnit!"

Tattoo and the
bulky airport guy were
closing in on me. I
staggered through the
trees, running straight
for Tattoo, turning
my head from time to
time to peer at Baldy

as if I didn't know he had friends. I felt like a dumbass scared girl in a bad horror flick.

Tattoo blocked my path with his wide bulk, the barrel of his gun pointed at my face. "I got you." He reached for my arm and I pulled it behind my back then swiveled my body and gulped hard as Baldy and Bulky closed in on me.

'What do you want?" I panted, my

voice shaky. My body in a defensive stance.

Bulky stepped forward as if he was the leader. He lowered his gun. "We need you to come with us." His deep voice rattled my inner senses into a frazzle. *Damn, he was hot!*

I shifted my eyes from him to the others and back to him. "You're the guy from the airport. I didn't do anything wrong. What do you want?"

Bulky glanced at the other guys and gestured for them to lower their weapons. "We're not going to hurt you, but you need to come with us," he urged, his silky eyes catching the moon's light. It was almost a full moon.

"You have guns. I have no weapons." If only they knew the strength in my jaw, the sharpness of my teeth and claws. "I'm defenseless."

Bulky shrugged and let out a low chuckle as if I was a simple, defenseless female. I threw him a death glance. "You think it's funny, preying on women alone in the woods, after being denied their flight?" I narrowed my eyes at Bulky to intensify my words.

Tattoo and Baldy grabbed hold of my

arms and dragged me
out of the woods. I
put up a believable
fight, tugging my
hands and kicking at
their shins. I freed
one arm and jerked
the other almost free
of his grasp. He
clutched firmer as it
slid through his
sweaty palms. His
fingers digging into
my flesh. "I'm not
who you think. I don't
know anything," I
whimpered through
conjured tears as

Tattoo wrapped his thick hand around my arm again.

As they stuffed me into the SUV, a small breeze rustled the treetops and brought an odor. It was too far for me to be sure, but it brought back a case of deja vu. Bulky pulled my hands behind my back and my feet together then wrapped them with plastic restraints as if I couldn't snap free. That was good.

It meant I truly wasn't
bound and they didn't
know I wasn't
anything other than
human.